STEVEY SMITH

A PLAY
BY
ULRICK YCZENIAPLAUS

Stevey Smith

A PLAY

Musical play mother fucker

BY

Ulrick Yczeniaplaus

A MUSICAL FUCKING PLAY FOR 2020 FUCK HEADS.

Wot is aslo serious fucking mother fucker.

This is an original fictional work. Any aspersions with, references to, resemblance to, or similarity with natural persons or legal entities is entirely coincidental, unintended and spurious.

As for factual quotes used from the public domain; do your own homework, lazy bones.

And don't fucking come to me and tell me I copied some shit. I only read shit in the public domain. So if three words together or whatever are the same as some fucking where else, fucking coincidence. I'm telepathic. I can read your fucking mind shitter. Come at me, and I'll be inside your head telling you what to do, you greedy useless lazy freeloading fucked up cunt.

A ONE ACT PLAY WITH MUSIC AT THE WISH OF THE DIRECTOR

Cast:-

Andy = A

Boris = B

Carl = C

Denny = D

Emma = E

Stevey Smith = S

Set:-
Open stage with large table and six chairs to the centre left. Long bench and table to the right. Old upright Piano and stool.
 Reverse red neon sign at the back 'CAFE YEKOW'
In the big window next to street door. The sign is on. Underneath the red neon 'OPEN' sign is off.

I hates to reminds yous peeps but- juts to make it fucking completely fucking clear and understoods, Stevey fucking plays the fucking piano good- right fucker? His singing fucking sucks though...

SCENE ONE

*S; sitting on the end chair facing audience alone.
He has a bag on the table.*

*S IS PLAYING PIANO alone some fucking tune he
likes. He stops and talks. Drinks coffee.*

S; I don't want to be here. I have never wanted to
be here. What I want, what I really, really want, is
to be there. I want. I demand. I deserve. I have
rights. I am right. I want to show everyone why I
am right and be there- one of many- a gang
member- a crewman- a party member- one of the
lads- a team player. With respect. With friends.
With brothers and sisters I can rely on. Speak to.

Feel at home with. My peer group clutch. Us
versus the world. We and them. We made our
plans, agreed them, and dove in. Hidden among
the sea of faces. Happy. Together. Players in the
great game. Past winners who will win again today.
Now.

Members of our own private club, secreted in the crowds. Working up and up to make our way. Standing on every head. Doing our tricks. Giving our secret signals to each other. Getting stuff done. Being real- being really alive- in one, great, big life party. Winning.

E: enters stage left and puts her bag on the table.

E: Stevey, my baby boy! What the fuck. You should be out there. Why are you here?

S; You think I know?

E; You think I know? (*sarcastic*)

S; Why are you here?

E; Because you are. I'm talking to you, Stevey baby boy.

Stands on the table, points with each word to S

E; You fucking useless cunt.

Sits down.

E; You imagine you're one of us? One of the crew?
One of the band? Ha ha ha ha ha- HA!
You useless shithead fuck. You're NO ONE. NO
ONE! A paper thin slice of shit out on the wind. A
zit zombie shitting cunt-sucker fuckhead.

S; *(stands)* Fuck you. Fuck you and fuck you and
fuck you very much, Emma. You cunt. You fucking
cunt. You fucked up fucking fuck cunt.

*They both laugh outrageously and slap each other
round the face over and over and over and say:-*

S; Fuck you.

E: Fuck you.

Until they get bored and red faced with the hits.

*S sits at the piano and starts playing 'Bridge over
Troubled Water' backwards in the wrong key.*

A enters thru the cafe front door

A: Whats with all the fucking fucks? I can hear you
from down the street through the traffic.

S and E: Fuck you, you fucking cunt.

A; Nice. Very nice. Emma, bring me a coffee for fuck's sake.

E; We're closed fucking cunt faced cunt. Closed. Not open. Shut. Not here. At fucking home.

A: Good.

A puts his bag on the table next to the others.

A; Now, fucking bring me a fucking coffee fucking fast you fucking fucked up fucking cunt faced cock sucker, and it better be the best fucking coffee you ever fucking made in your fucking fucked up fucking shitty life. Cock. Sucker.

E; Fuck you.

E; leaves stage left.

A; sits down at the table an so does S.

S; What are you doing?

A; I'm sending a fucking text. Any problems with that mother fucker?

S; No, fucker. I want to be out there. With the others. Out in the real world.

A; So what the fuck are you doing here then fucker?

S; Fucking talking to you.

A; So stay here now. I do want to to talk to you before you fuck off.

Text message beeps from amongst the audience. Boris, Carl and Denny read their messages and stand up from random locations in seats in the audience.

B, C & D: Fuck you you fucking cunts. Fuck you and fuck you all and fucking fuck the fuck out of you.

SCENE TWO

B,C & D go onto the stage and confront A. They put their bags on the table.

B, C & D: What the fuck you do that for? You fucked in the head, Andy?

B; I had two beepers credit cards already.

C; I got a nice fat bag.

D; I have two wallets full of plastic and... $280.

A; Fucking fantastic. Fucking A. Fucking peanuts. Now, listen fuckers. We is moving up and up. This is it. Now. We all been waiting for this. Now I got the stuff to make it happen. We got the whole fucking chocolate bar stuffed full of peanuts in one lump. In sight. Full fucking spunk load.

B, C & D: Wah. Fucking A.
They sit at the table.

S; Fuck this. I want to be out there. Put me out there Andy you fucker.

A; Fuck off loser. That's yesterday. Today is fucking today. Today is now. Today is us fuckers here fucking those mother fucking cunts out there like they never been fucking fucked before. We is going to be the magicians, cleaning the underwear off their fucking hot stinking corpses without even touching the fuckers.

S; How the fuck are we going to do that mother fucker?

A: Stevey boy, there is places and times for some things, and other places and times for other fucking things. You want to go out there, go fucker. Go and don't fucking bother coming back. Going out there is fucking 1984. Its Wellington. Napoleon. Hitler, Mussolini. Churchill. USSR. Its Vietnam. Iraq. Afghanistan. Its Ebola. Covid19. Cancer. Its motherfucking war, with plague, with every shitter focused on shitting on you. It's the fucking killing fields in 2020. Protest, arrest, Portland, Shooting, Death and destruction. Let me ask you- what is that mother fucker? You agree with me- its fucking past you fucker. Done with. Over. Fucked and fucking dead.

S; But the cities thrive on hate and shitting. That's all they have. Hate and shitting. Its been like that for as long as everyone can recall. What the fuck reason makes any change for today? What's so fucking special about now? The whole fucking city runs of evil shitting motherfuckers. You expect them to wake up and say; 'Oh, you know what, I'm gonna change my fucking ways today. Yeah. Yeah. It's mother fucking today. Let's all start right now. Let me call my crew and we'll mother fucking bin our tin and go aerial social. We'll put it on the radio. The TV. The net. Today's the day we drop the beef and eat mother fucking quiche.' Who in their right mind who ain't gots a death fucking wish is gonna do that shit, huh?

E comes in with coffee and nasty, serves every one.

E; Fuck this. Fuck this. I can't hear no more. Stop it. Stop it now. My ears are burning, burning, burning. (*Screams*).

A; You're right, Emma. Your fucking right. This is too much. Every breath, every step, every thought. Now, its thoughts they want to control as well as everything else. What the fuck is left for us, huh? Nothing. We got nothing. Nothing. No life. No future. No past worth a mother fucking cent.

S; What's this wonder fuck you got now, eh, fucker? What is it Andy, that I can't go and fucking fuck the fuckers? Like we all been doing for fucking as long as I remember. Like I want to fuck off the cafe and go out fucking the fuck of the fucks.

A; You fucking spit in this coffee fucker Emma? Did you fucking spit in my coffee again?

E; No. No way. Fuck off.

A gets up and wallops E. She cries. A sits, gets out a small water bottle from his bag and drinks.

A: You got to fucking learn some fucking manners, Emma you fuck faced cunt sucker.

E; From who? From you, cunt face?

All throw their coffee at Emma.

A; Get some fucking proper coffee. Now you fucking low life piece of shit cunt sucker bitch.

E leaves stage left.

S; Yeah Emma. Get some fucking manners on you cunt.

A; Shut the fuck up Stevey.

B: So what's the deal Andy?

C: Yeah. Whats the big fuck?

D; Yeah. Tell us. Show us now you fucker, or are you just waving your chops in the brown bowl?

S; You're lying through your fucking teeth, Andy. You just want to get a fuck on us today and rip us the way you usually do. With your brown bowl cunt sucking tongue. You get off on it. You enjoy tongue wiping ass you fucking mother fucking fucker.

A smacks S in the mouth. S sits down.

A: Nah. Today is real. Today, I made it. Today, I fixed what I started before we was fucking cunts. Today, I put my hand down with a full house. A hand I been playing since before there was a before. It's fucking mother fucking real, ok stink shit brown bowl fuckers?
Today, I know I is the human animal I was born as. Here is the fucking proof. It's real. It's proof that we are real. That we are fucking human, not fucking mother fucking bits of economy. Parts of fucking money plans. We is not fucking paperwork, numbers, digits. We is people, with

blood and hearts and life and death. One life. One death. We was born people, and we'll fucking die people. Not machines, fucking stats, fucking brown bowling stock fucking market indices. We- you, me, all of us- we is people. Shitbook, Rivershit Tockfucking tick, We tube, Flecknix, Grandma Instant, and Mr fuckface can all go get brown bowled.

They want every fucking breath you take. Know where you is every second so they can sell you want they want you to buy, at their prices, from them. They tell you what you want, what you need, what you have to do, to comply to be 'one of them', fuckers. @ Don't use that café. It's shit there. Use this new one that's reeeeeeeeal nice. Blah blah fucking blah. This is fucking money lifestyle preaching every fucking brown bowling fucking second of every fucking day and night. They are fucking 1984. They are big brother. Them shitters is selling our fucking souls for nothing, without even getting out fucking permission. That's fucking us. That's who we are. That's the fucking system we made for our lovely lives today. Being, no- beings made for machines to make fucking money. For the shitters.

B; So what's the plan then Andy- go fucking Quaker? Live off the land a drive around in buggies with fucking horses?

C; You want we dump the fucking system and go get green paint and make the fucking city green, bro? Is that the fucking way? Have a man standing at every junction saying when to stop and go?

A; That would be something to see.

D; Yeah. I get one thing, too. I is talking with my buddies, and the shitters are tapping in, they know who spoke with who and when, for how long, and maybe even the things we spoke about. They know. Its all information. Free for them. Some fucking It shitter is looking at a hundred million calls and playing with the data. Yeah, the shitter says, that's them talking about the game. Its that time. Between the halves.
They- they look at each email, too. They check each fucking word. If I write an email – or a text- about my health, next I know I get fifty emails advertising health and medical shit. They look at everything you do. Everything. Then, they tell you, 'Oh, your shit's no good. You need to buy our shit. It's fucking better. Yours is old. Yours is bad. Yours is not fucking fashionable. Your shit is out of date.

Go, get a loan and buy our better new up-to-date shit now.

All; (Laugh). Fuck them shitters.

All sit back silent in questioning disbelief. Emma arrives with fresh coffee and serves it around.

E; This is fucking good,ok fuckers?

A; Nice. You drink it Emma. Drink from this cup. Show everyone how good it is.

Emma pours a full one, downs it in A's face.

S drinks his down.

S; Ahhh.

A; Well aint we the happy fucking cunting couple cafe fuckers. What you do next? Suck each other's asses with a fat fucking smile and great big 'Ahh'? Tell me, Stevey, who goes on top, and who gets the runny side up?

S & E: Fuck you.

E; You never had a father to hate. Fuck you.

S: You never had a mother to fuck. You had to down anyone else's. Fuck you.

A; I did what I did and that's past. You can make what mind fucks you want. I'm not here today to play games. This-

He pulls his bag on the table to him and opens the flap so they all look and see something inside.

-Is real.
A drinks coffee while watching the others.

B; That's not real.

C; That's not real.

D; That's not fucking real.

A; So if its not fucking real, then what the fuck is it? A juicy brown bowl?

B; Nah. Nah. Nah.

C; Where this come from?

D; How d'you get it?

E; Who did you fuck to get this shit?

S; You mother fucking murdering cunt. I know where this came from. I know. I seen it before. This is nothing. Nothing. You fucking got off on it for nothing. Its fake. Its a copy. Its what you are, Andy, a lying mother fucking piece of shit.

A finishes his coffee get up and walks around.

A; You think lies and copies is what this is, Stevey boy? And what about this? All this here. Is this true? How do you measure a lie if its all fucking lies? If there's fucking nothing left that's true.

If everything you ever knew turns out to be in the sweet, brown bowl? What fucking yardstick do you use then, eh, fuckboy? The least lying one? A mix? A golden mother fucking pick'n'mix choice from all of them? Do you start small and change the lies as you go along, arrive at the lying mother fucking answer lie and say, 'yes, this lie I can live with. This lie, I can die for'.

You make the mother fucking rules now, eh, Stevey boy? Pick your lie well, and tell us all about

it. Pick it and make it stand up. Give it fucking legs
and a heart to believe in.

Come on mother fucker. We're all waiting for you
to make us gasp at your truth. All standing around
with out tails open and plans ready at the cross
roads.
Put your fucking hand on it. Smell it. Feel it. Taste
it. Use your fucking senses and tell me what it isn't.
Then, tell me what it fucking is.

B; It don't matter. It don't matter its not real. The
whole fucking fuck is a lie. It's what we believe. Its
what we believe makes it real.

C & D: I believe it's real.
E; So its real. So now what? Lie its fucking way into
heaven? Lie its real lying fucking way off the
shithole and up and up?

S; I'm hungry. That's a truth. It's raining out there
somewhere. That's a truth. I'm alive. That's a
fucking truth. There is truth. Truth fucking exists.
Just like lies do. Truth is as real as lies are.

A; And how much truth did we win today, eh?
Boris? Hmm? Put it out.

B and all put their shit on the table and spread it.

B; Hmm... Maybe three-four grand all in.

A; Maybe three-four grand. All in. Haah. That's some mighty big truth right there fuck heads. One mighty fucking world changing big truth of it all. Three or four grand. A fucking good day.

E; Money ain't truth. Truth is truth. Money is money.

S; Oh yeah. Oh fucking A yeah. Truth is what you believe. Truth can change from, from one minute to the next. Now, it's sunny, now, it's raining.

A; So Stevey boy, what you is saying is that truth is small. The weather is big, and the truth of the weather changes as times passes along. Is that it?

S; Well, yeah. Yeah. Like that.

A; So, is it true to say the fucking weather changes all the fucking time then? Come fucking rain or shine, it's fucking changing every fucking second of every fucking day?

S; Yeah. Like that.

A; So big things, like the weather, can be true too as well as small things? Is that it too?

E; Yeah. Yeah.

A; And where the fuck does this truthful weather all fucking come from then?

S; From nature. Nature makes the weather.

A; Anyone disagree with that? Oh. Good. We found ourselves another mother fucking truth right there. Nature makes the weather. The great, big, world changing weather that rains or shines as it feels like.

B; Where the fuck is this fucking thinking going, Andy. We could be out there making money, and we're here talking about the fucking weather.

A; You want to know where this fucking major league baseball conversation is going to end up Boris?

B; Yeah. Time is money.

A; Time is fucking money. Is that what you believe or is that the truth, huh?

B; Both. When I is working, I is making money. By using my time that way.

A; You believe that, huh?

B; Yeah. It's fucking true.

S; You is part of nature, Boris, right? So you is part of time. Time is made by nature. That you make money with your time is a choice, not a truth. When you make your choices, like when you is working, then the truth is, you is working because you want- not because something NOT you put you there. You did it.

B; Huh? What the fuck I did?

A; Like...Like fishing. Like fucking fishing for fish in the river. The fish live in the river. You go to the river to catch fish. If you go to the mountains, to the mall, to the- the car park, the street, there ain't no fish there.

B; What the fuck you talking about fishing for?

C: One minute ago it was talking about the weather. Now its fucking fish.

D; And nature. What the fuck has nature got to do with any of us?

S; See all those mother fucking cunts out there, Denny? See all those mother fucking people fucking hanging around doing what ever they do? When I get out there, I can fish those mother fucking cunts. I can get the fucking golden trout in and win, Dub. If I don't get to fucking go, I cant do shit. That's the nature of it. That's the truth of it.

A; You do see the choices, Stevey boy. That's true.

S; That's true? You get it now, Boris?

B; Yeah. I guess. When I choose to do something, it's only true when I am doing it as my choice. Not as a fact outside my choice. Right? Or something. I can say like, 'I did that', after, and that would be true if I had done that. But, my ass working is my choice, and not like, the rain.

S; So what the fuck is this fucking shit of a lie in your bag on the table here, Andy? This copy? This fucking fake shit that's worth a fucking glass eye in some fucking swimming pool?

A; Ho now, you talk about eyes. You talk about seeing. You talk about swimming pools. I think you know the answer to your own question, Stevey boy. It sounds as if you get the point to your own opinion. It sounds like you know what is and for us, you is spinning out a lie like a fucking fat fucking spider web to us all here. Where the fuck will that take you, huh?
Tell me.

S; I- I don't know. I wanted to go out there, That's all. I wanted to be working on the team. Not here waiting and fucking serving organic fair-sourced coffee and fat free fucking vegan doughnuts.

E; You are part of the team, Stevey boy.

B; Yeah.

C; You know it.

D; You is family, bro. Family. Like the youngest. You do your stuff, it's just as strong as we do.

A; Yeah. You're still a fucking fucked up fucking cunt though.

All laugh except S. D gets up on the table and drops the back of her pants to show her naked ass away from the audience for her mooning at S. She grasps her buttocks and moves them in time to her speech.

D; Hey, Stevey. You want to go out there and be a man today, huh? Do a bit of brown bowling work, fucker? OO-oo. OO-oo. OO-oo.

D sits down again. All laugh and some hoot including S.

C; Oh yeah baby. Oh yeah. Tell it like it is hahaha.

B; Get me a better seat, Denny. I missed some of those long words.

E; You're so full of shit, Denny. Really full. I saw. Hahaha.

D; Got me a long one comin'. Wanna see, huh?

A; See, Stevey? We're all family here, boy. You. Me. All one big happy fucking fucked up mother fuckin' family bro.

S; I seen. I seen. It's true. It's lies. I seen. What the fuck? What I want to know the fuck is- is what it fucking <u>means,</u> Andy.

A; Ho ho ho, Stevey boy. Ho ho ho.

A does 4 slow hand claps.

All; Ho ho ho.

All 4 x slow hand claps.

A; Half a fucking hour and you hit the bomb button big fucking bang. Listen to the man, sluts. Listen to the one of us has half a fucking brain. Took me fucking all my time to get that. All my fucking time- 'what does it mean'?

Yeah, Stevey boy, that's the fucking nut cracker. What the fuck does it MEAN- eh? Fuck the lies. Fuck the truth. It's a fucking box of cereal twisters. Or not. It don't matter none fucker. It's a pony. It's a plane. It's a phone. It's a fucking whatever you want it to fucking be. The only fucking question worth any fucking salt here- is what the fuck does it mean?

S; Yeah. Yeah. So. What does it mean...

All: Tell us fuck head, tell us, what the fuck it means?

S gets up and walks around.

S; ... I dunno. I dunno what the fuck it fucking means. I know, I know it means something. Something I don't know now. Fucking something without lies or truth. Something... fucking different.

All: Something different.

A; Going my way, fuck head. Going my way. All the shit. All the fucking crap and lies and shitty shitter shit and crap. All of it. Life. It's all shit. Crap.

Strung high dog turds dryin' in the RAIN.
Every fucking day's the mother fucking same.

All; Every mother fucking day's the mother fucking same.

S; Yeah. Yeah. Sitting and waiting. Yeah. The same shit every day. Sitting and fucking waiting.

All: Shitting and pissing it every mother fucking single day. Shitting on the piss of your life away.

A; You got it, Stevey boy. You got it. It's all a big, juicy brown bowl of creamy shit.

S; And this- this is different?

A; Yep. Its fucking something else, fuck head.

All: This isn't shit? It isn't fucking lies with extra fucking creamy crap on top?

A; OK. OK. Put your hands in the bag, sluts.

They all do except E, who holds back. A grabs her hand and shoves it in the bag.

A; What d'you feel,huh... tell me, tell me -what d'you fucking feel?

B; I don't feel fucking nothin'. It's cold. Smooth...

C; That's the back of my fucking hand fuck head.

B; Oh. Yeah. Too many fucking hands.

E; It feels... like... a fucking weird thing. Like something fucking new. Not money. Not gold. Fucking weird.

All; It feels fucking weird.

A; Yep. Look. That there something, is a fucking weird thing, not a something.

The all look round at A and take their hands out from the bag. E carefully inspects her hand held in front of her face
All; Its a fucking weird fucking thing.

E; It's ... it's the truth. It's true. It's real. It's nature. Like the weather. It's like fucking raining. On my hand.

All; It's not a fucking lie. It's the fucking weirdest thing - true. It's not a fucking lie. It's fucking weirdness fucking over you.

S: I don't fucking get it.

A; You supposed to huh?

S; No. No. But maybe I fucking could get it... if I... if I...

All: If you fucking what?

S; Nah. I don't like it. It's fucking weird. I don't like it. Lets fuck it. Now.

All; Fuck it. Fuck it. Fucking fuck it anyhow.

We're gonna fucking fuck it right fucking now.
It's mother fucking weird.
Fucking fuck it anyhow.

A; And then what?

S; What 'then what'?

A; Fuck it because its weird? Fuck it because right now, you don't fucking understand it? Is that it? Do you understand the fucking weather, huh? Why not fuck that first. It's fucking been fucking us all for as long as we know. Do you know how life is made, sluts, huh?

All; No.

A; OK. Something lower down your fuck heads. Do you know how to farm rice, huh?

All; No.

A; Fucking Jesus H fucking Ker-ist. Lower… Do you know what makes coffee from beans, huh?

All; No.

A; Don't fucking know fucking much, do you, sluts. Why not fuck all that weird stuff first?

S; Coffee's been around for as long as I can recall. Like the fucking weather.

A; Yeah. Sure. But that's why you accept it even though you don't fucking understand it. It's not weird to you at all?

All; No.

S; Because it's how it is. It's how it's always been. It's how it's always going to fucking be.

A; Are you sure about that? What if the farmers all fucking stopped growing coffee beans today, huh? No more fucking coffee.

S; Yeah. That would be weird.

A; Yeah. That would be fucking weird.

All; Yeah Fucking weird.

A; So, just because something is weird, don't mean it's gots to be fucked. Whose going fuck all the coffee bean farmers, eh, sluts? You gonna spend the rest of your mother fucking lives going round every single coffee bean farmer and fucking them, huh? And, then, whose gonna fucking go out there and fuck the weather, huh? No one, that's who, huh?

E; What about fucking climate change?

A; Who the fuck cares about climate change. You think the planet gives a fuck about the climate? You think there's a fucking climate to worry about on the fucking moon mother fucker?

E; Yeah but we live here.

A: Yeah. We live here. You know about fucking science now, huh, slut? Nothing about fucking your fucking coffee that is your fucking business- but all about the fucking planet? Ooooo. Its not some fucking weird shit no one understands?

All; The whole mother fucking planet's a fucking real weird hole.

A: Right. It's all fucking fucked up weird shit. I'll tell you what I understand, and you tell me how wrong I am. We warm up the fucking planet. More CO2 in the air. The weather gets more extreme. More sun. More wind. More rain. That means less ice and snow. Then guess fucking what? You fuck heads just guess the fuck what, eh? Go on.

PAUSE in thoughtful Silence.

Well?

Second pause with some foot stomps and 'Errs'.

A; This is what. We stop the next fucking ice age from happening is what.

All; The next what?

A; The next fucking ice age. When the planet gets too cold and it freezes over and everybody dies.

E; What? So when is that going to fucking happen? Tomorrow? Next year? Next 100 years?

A; Aha. Ah fucking ha. Put your hands on the weird thing. Go on. All you sluts. Do it. Fucking do it now. Ask your question to yourself, 'When is the fucking next ice age on Earth'?

They all put their hands in the bag for a minute. Silence. E draws her hand out first and checks her mobile phone. She reads, and all watch her languidly drawing out their hands one by one.

E: Fuck. Fuck. Fuck. Listen to this shit.
It says, "The change in sunlight associated with the ice age cycles is quite subtle and takes thousands of years to make a difference to temperatures and to ice gain or loss.
"When atmospheric carbon dioxide is above about 300 parts per million, the infrared warming effect is so strong it drowns out the more subtle Milan-ko-vitch cycles and there are no ice ages.

"Coming out of the Pli-o-cene period just under three million years ago, carbon dioxide levels dropped low enough for the ice age cycles to commence.

"Now, carbon dioxide levels are over 400 parts per million and are likely to stay there for thousands of years, so the next ice age is postponed for a very long time.

"We will be living in a warmed and changed
climate for many generations to come."
Fuck. That's just so fucking weird.

S; Yeah. Yeah. Fucking weird.

A; Yeah. Fucking fucked up mother fucking weird.

B; Ah, it's all fucking shit. Fucking juicy brown bowl
sucking fucking fucked up shit. We have to stop
the climbing change or we're fucked.

A; Really?

B; Yeah. Really, fucker? How you know this fucking
internet shit Emma just said is the truth, huh?
Maybe it's just another cock sucking shitter lying
to the world, huh?

A; Oh. Yeah. Big fucking shit. This cock sucker who
wrote that shit, dont have a penny to make from it.
He's fucking saying the opp-o-site of the climbing
changers. He got his cock out, waved it around all
over, measured it against the CO2 levels in the air,
and wrote it the fuck down, bro. OK?

B; He got his cock out?

A; Yeah.

B; And sniffed the fucking air?

A; Yeah.

B; I believe the climbing changers, though.

A; Oh. Do you now, huh? And who fucking told you that shit then, huh? I'll tell you who told you. Some mother fucking juicy brown bowling greedy raping cock sucker, that's who.

S; Yeah. Yeah. I can feel it. I can feel it. I can feel the planet. I can fucking feel the fucking planet fucker. It's telling me to go fuck myself.

All: We can feel the fucking planet fuckers.
Go and fucking fuck yourself.
Go and fucking fuck yourself,
And grow a new dick for the Spring.

B; I'm learning to swim.

C; I'm gonna grow me tomatoes.

D; I'm gonna steal me the warmest Winter clothes I can find.

A; Nah. Nah, Denny. There ain't gonna be no
fucking ice age, bro.

SCENE THREE

All: No ice age? No Ice age. No ice age.

They jump around the stage shouting over and over.

All: No ice age. No ice age. No ice age.
Oh...
No ice age. No ice age. No ice age.
Ho...

E; But what about fucking sea levels going up. My brother lives in Queens. It'll be under water.

A; It is what it is, Emma. It is what it is. Where we are today, and where we'll be tomorrow, is what will be. Maybe he'll have to move. Maybe he'll get a fucking boat. Maybe he'll be a seaweed farmer. Who the fuck knows?

And. And. For what:- Do you think that some fuckers are never gonna bring on fusion power and solar power and wind power? Its fucking cheaper than coal or gas. Its clean. Its climate fucking friendly. 400 parts of CO2 per million in the air is where we are now. It's cheaper. Tell me if I'm wrong mother fucker- listen:- Do you know any fucking shitter who spends more money than they has to? No- right. They do what's cheaper-

All; Cheaper- yeah.

A; -Spend less, make more- out do their competitors, do it big, do it cheap, and guess the fuck what- they do it just to make more money. Make more profits. That's big time shitter business, bro. Chasing the dollarios. Making the ming. Chopping the crap.

All; Saving money- yeah.

A: Look the fuck where we came from before 100 fucking years, bro, we was using fucking candles. Candles! And horses! Every fucking shitter on the road was Wild ridin' fucking Bill Big Cock!

All; Candles. Horses. What a fuck up.

A; In a few hundred years from now, our tech will be so fucking strong, so advanced, so mother fucking clever, so clean, so cheap, it'll replace all the old fucked up expensive CO2 making power stations and sea levels will be fine. Just fucking fine. Hahahaha. Unless we get hit by a mother fucking asteroid first. Hahahaha.

All; Hit me with your mother fucking asteroid fucker. Hit me. Hit me!

E; So what's all this shit about fucking climbing change then?

S; Its all fucking lies. Its lies. All fucking fucked up mother fucking scare the living shit from all the shitters lies. To get money. To pay taxes. To sell books. So fucking mother fuckers can get paid shit loads of cash to do fuck all, talk shit, get grants and teaching jobs for nothing. Fucking free money for fucking nothing.

All; Fucking mother fucking fuckers.

A; Yeah, sea levels will go up some. But not by much. You see any fucking mother fucking billionaires selling all their sea shore lake side properties, huh? No.

All; Nah.

A; Nah. Not fucking one of them. They're fucking buying. They're fucking buying more and building more and investing more in beach and lake real estate. Prices are on the up and up.

All; Prices are on the up and up. Greedy cunts are buying all the shit. Sluts. Sluts. Sluts.

E; We been sold a fucking lie. And been forced to fucking pay for it.

All; All the fucking lies. We bought all the fucking lies. Bought and paid for with our blood and fucking addict's highs.

S goes to piano and plays accompaniment and they all crowd round and sing:

All;
We all got fucking fucked
by clever fucking cunts.
Mother fucking greedy
useless fucking cunts.
They lied. They lied,
they fucking stole and lied.
They fucking stole our lives
and lied until we died.
E;
Give me all your money now
you fucking shitting dirt.

C; Here.
Take my fucking salary.
My car- and take my shirt.
I don't need them anymore.
We're saving us the planet

By renting asses at my door.

All;
We all got fucking fucked by clever fucking cunts.
Mother fucking greedy useless fucking cunts.
They lied. They lied, they fucking stole and lied.
They fucking stole our lives and lied until we died.

E gets more coffee for everyone and they all sit at the table.

S; What I don't get is…

A falls on the floor in surprise.

S; What I don't get is why we let these cunts fuck us over like this? All the fucking do-nations. The lies. The fucking lies to get money.

A; (*from the floor*) Stevey boy. What you are doing now is… (*he gets up*) asking… a… question.

All; What you mean- a question?

A; Its what we ask when we're supposed to shut the fuck up, drop our pants and take it with a smile like good brown bowl boys.

C; Aha.

E; And I want to ask a fucking question. I want to ask. Now.

All; We're all ears mother fucker. Ask away.

E; Can we fucking cancel these fucking cunts? I want them all canceled. CANCEL. You know how much fucking cash I gave these fuckers? You know how much?

All; How much?

S; She gave them all she had.
They stripped her of her dignity
and took every cent she had.
All; That's mother fucking mad.
That's mother fucking bad.

E; I'm fucking naked on the floor.
Smiling as they fuck my ass
and rape on me some more.

S goes to the piano and plays.

All;
These fucking cunts are rapists
They rape and steal and lie.

These fucking cunts are rapists
They trashed our fucking dignit-I
And smiled while waving you 'good bye'.

S; She gave them all she had.
They stripped her of her dignity
and took every cent she had.
All; That's mother fucking mad.
That's mother fucking bad.

E; I'm fucking naked on the floor.
Smiling as they fuck my ass
and rape on me some more.

All;
These fucking cunts are rapists
They rape and steal and lie.
These fucking cunts are rapists
They trashed our fucking dignit-I
And you smiled very wishing them 'good bye'.

*Apart from S who continues to play, they all make
a conga line and go round the stage making fucks
up each others asses, singing,*

All;
Lets all fuck our asses
Lets all fuck our asses
Its best to do
Its best to do
Lets all fuck our asses
Lets all fuck our asses
They said its true
They said its true.
Lets all fuck our asses
Lets all fuck our asses
The cunts want you
They want you too.
Lets all fuck our asses
Lets all fuck our asses
Its best to do
Its best to do
Lets all fuck our asses
Lets all fuck our asses
They said its true
They said its true.
Lets all fuck our asses
Lets all fuck our asses
The cunts want you
They want you too.

All sit down in a pandemonium of face slaps and
'Fuck you mother fuckers, ~sluts, and ~cunts', *until*
they get settled down.

D; This question asking thing…its fucking up 'n' up.
I like it.

B; I fucking got one. I got one- ok fuckers? Why
is… what we do… criminal… and what they do…
legal?

D; Because we're fucking scum sluts mother
fucker. We're worthless shit slits of street scum
mother fuckers who no one will miss if we die any
fucking time at all. That's why.

B; Oo. This is fucking good shit. A fucking answer.
To my quest-i-on. I like it.

C; Can anyone ask a question? Like fucking any
fucking mother fucker at all? Like me?

A; You can ask any fucking question you fucking
like. To anyone. At anytime. Just don't expect a
mother fucker to give you an answer that makes
any sense. They're all mother fucking lying cunts.
They're more likely to use the chance to fuck you
up the ass.

S; I got one. I got one… this is a good fucker. How many… how many people have … fucking… lived and died before us then? Lived and got through life and fucking died before now, right? For us to be here talking like the mother fucking cunts we are?

A; Ah. This is a good one for fucking sure. Emma?

E; The internet says… it says… "Over the last 50,000 years, 100 billion. Lived and died". A best guess.

All; Fuck.

S; So over the last million years then, including the last 50,000 years, maybe ten times that, eh?

E; Maybe… one minute…no, I cant find that. Only some references to a volcanic eruption in Asia about 75,000 years ago called Lake Toba in Sumatra, where ever the fuck that is, that is thought to have affected human life so badly that the world population was dropped to about 10,000 or so then, all in East Africa.

C; Wow. 10,000 people. That's less than the town I grew up in. You mean, in the whole world?

E; Yeah. That's what it says.

All; Fuck.

B; How you know what they write is so though. It could be a crock.

E: There is a lot of ev-i-dence. Too much scientific archaeology and shit. Its all full here. Full of it. They found graves. Bones. Not just human, animals, too. They looked at the layers in soil all over the planet. Listen.

"On balance, the evidence is so heavy in favour of carefully discovered scientific proof that at this time in pre-history there was an 'extinction event', the chance of this not being the case can no longer be considered defendable."

B; Fuck. Defend-able. Fuck. These cunts are so fucking clever.

E; Yeah 10,000 or so fucking people in the whole fucking world. Sterk Fountain. Blomberg. Echo. More. All these shit caves full of ancient crap. In South fucking Africa.

C; I left my home town coz I is gay and no one else was. I don't put out. I don't slide the streets renting mother fucker. I has me self respectiblazes.

And I respect straights and kids just coz they can do what they want like I do what I want. I don't tell them the fuck what to fucking think. What to fucking do. What to fucking say. I don't put on them. Shit, if I do that to you fuck heads, what you do, huh?

All; We tell you to go fuck yourself, fuck head!

C; And right, too. You is you and me is me and we is WE-E-E. Right?

All; Fucking right mother fucker. The fuck head family of WE-E-E.

B; Still, who can believe this internet shit, eh? It's all crap. They put any fucking shit on the internet and every moron shitter fucking believes it. It's sure fucking crap. Like that shit about climbing change. It is or it isn't total crap. It's like, the shitters take some shit, and don't tell you the whole story. Just what they want you to know, so they can fuck us up the mother fucking ass.

S; Yeah. Any fucking shit they like and TELL us what to fucking think.

B; Yeah. Fuck that. The whole of all fucking humans was black one time in Africa? All the fucking same? Just 10,000 of our...an-cest-ors?

All;
All the fucking same.

B; Why is... why is the fucking whole fucking world putting on me coz I is black huh? I is one of the fucking family. I aint fucking diffrent. I is the fucking same as all of you and you and you.

A; Yeah, good one, Boris. We is all the fucking same.

E; Yeah. And... and... this religion shit. We is right, they is wrong. They is wrong. We is right. That aint fucking no God talking. There aint no God watching me to make sure I take a dump the right fucking way or else. That's fucking shitters that is, grabbing for power mother fucker. Standing on my fucking head and pissing down my fucking shit while they rape my sorry brown bowl ass and steal every fucking penny I got. None of that's respectiblazes. It's all a complete fucking crock of mother fucking shit.

All; Yeah right mother fucker.

A; Yeah. Wear these fucking clothes, fucker. Stand like this. Sit like this. Kneel here, mother fucker, and give me your fucking money.

All; Hahahaha.

C; That's fucking Boris working shitters, that is.

S; So lets be realistic then. Let me see if I get this right. OK? Today, there are all these shitters fucking us up the ass with their lies, and they expect us to play along and live our lives to their shit sucking rules they fucking impose on us while they fuck us over and over and THEN make us die for them, eh?

A; That's about the way of it, yeah.

All; Fucking mother fucking cunts.

S; I don't like it. I don't like it one fucking bit so fucking tiny you cant see it, feel it or smell it.

They're all a bunch of fucking cunts. They deserve
to fucking get fucked and die.

All; Yeah. Fuck em all.

S goes to the piano and plays tune.

All;
Fuck them all. Fuck them all.
They grab us and they pin us up against the wall.
They fucking fuck us up the ass
every time they come to pass.
Fucking mother fuckers, fucking fuck them all.
Fuck them all. Fuck them all.

They look for us like stupid rabbits
Fucking playing in their fields.
Every time we raise our heads
its then they fucking stab us
Just as they fucking feel
Stab and shoot and kill us dead.

Fuck them all. Fuck them all.
Its the power of the hour
that wins at every fucking turn.
We're their fucking ass hole flowers
Here only to get burned.

Fuck them all. Fuck them all.
They stand on us on every day.
Like they're a pyramid of power
They get on top and kill us any way.
Who gives any flying fuck for us- we're runts
They take everything they can- hooray-
And fuck us on the hour (bong)
Because we fucking let them cunts
Fucking fucking fuck us 'til we fucking fall.

We're the cunts. We're the cunts.
We're the fucking mother fucking fucking cunts.
We're the cunts. We're the cunts.
We fucking let them fuck us because we're the
fucking cunts.

We're the cunts. We're the cunts.
We're the fucking mother fucking fucking cunts.
We're the cunts. We're the cunts.
We fucking let them fuck us because we're the
fucking cunts.

Fuck them all. Fuck them all.
They grab us and they pin us up against the wall.
They fucking fuck us up the ass
every time they come to pass.
Fucking mother fuckers, fucking fuck them all.

They go and stand centre stage in line.

S;
Question. What if we stopped. Just stopped.

All;
Just stopped being fucked up the ass every fucking hour of every fucking day?

E; Yeah.

All; Yeah. Yeah. Yeah.

A; What happens if we stop getting fucked up the ass? What next? Where the fuck does that go?

E; Questions… questions… questions. What the fuck. You're fucking my head in.

D; I have something. I know about pain. I know about confusion. I know about mother fuckers. I fucking know about shit. And most in between.

*S goes to the piano and plays. D stands centre
stage and sings alone.*

I'm a man. I'm a man.
I would hardly know it but I am.
I'm a man. I'm a man.
I put my fucking cock on
Just because I can.

I used to be a girl
Like Emma is today
I used have big titties
That stuck out all the way

Then something fucking changed
Inside my fucking head
And the girl I knew as Denny
woke up one day quite dead.

I'm a man. I'm a man.
I would hardly know it but I am.
I'm a man. I'm a man.
I put my fucking cock on
Just because I can.

My cunt was juicy golden
boys chased me every chance
Young straight gay or olden
I got them all to dance.

I'm a man. I'm a man.
I would hardly know it but I am.
I'm a man. I'm a man.
I put my fucking cock on
Just because I can.

Now I had the plastic.
Now I had the ops.
Now I'm big and hairy
With a cock to call the cops.

I'm a man. I'm a man.
I would hardly know it but I am.
I'm a man. I'm a man.
I put my fucking cock on
Just because I can.

I'll fuck any fucked up bitch
Because its what I do.
I'll fuck every mother fucker
Cunt or ass or blew.

I'm a man. I'm a man.
I would hardly know it but I am.
I'm a man. I'm a man.
I put my fucking cock on
Just because I can.

There is one little problem
That I don't understand.
I should be fucking happy
That I got all I want at hand.

I'm a man. I'm a man.
I would hardly know it but I am.
I'm a man. I'm a man.
I put my fucking cock on
Just because I can.

S; I see fucker. I see.

They sit down again.

All; yeah, Denny. We all know this shit. Big wow.

D; This is the one minor teeny tiny issue fuckers.

A; Like fucking what?

D; I ain't happy, see. And I should be. I'm so fucked up, I don't know if its me or someone else. Who am I? What am I? I don't know who 'me' is.

A; Ok. Ok. OK. Ok. Ok. Ok. I fucking got it. Let me think…let me fucking just fucking think…

C; Go on, Andy, you'll see something new.

B; Yeah, go Andy. Put it on like how you do.

E: You donts got it.

S; He gots it.

E; He donts gots it.

S; He gots it.

E; He - don't- gots - it – fucker.

S: He fucking does tooo gots it fucking mother fucking bitch fucker gots it.

E &S face slap each other about.

A; Wait! Wait! Ok…listen. What about this. Just lets try this, ok?

All; OK…

A; Denny, who is fucking family, right? Right?

All; Right…

A; Denny changed from being a girl into a boy. Because he wanted to- right?

All; Right.

A; And Denny wasn't happy being a girl. And he thought he would be when he changed into being a boy, right so far- huh?

All; Right.

D; Right. Go on….

A; But, for some reason he don't know, he's not happy truly... not really... for what he is. Is that the truth of it Denny?

D; Yeah. Right.

A; So...its no good changing back to being a girl. Fucking done that. Been there. Flew the fucking kite and popped all the fucking balloons.

D; Yeah. Right.

A; So what I don't get is... what is you fucking expecting from changing from being a girl to being a boy? Or for that fucking matter, changing from being a boy into a girl?

D; I was... expecting to be... to be... happy. To be loved. Everyone- all the girls- and men- coming to me and saying how wonderful I was. Giving me their attention all the time. Making me feel so, so special.

A; Right, Right. You was the fucking princess in the fucking dream, huh? The fucking baby idea you had, that if this and that, the whole fucking world would fucking fall at your fucking feet as YOU- YOU became a fucking A list shitter- right?

D; Right.

A; And the change didn't make one fucking shit worth of difference, right? I dont see no fucking queues of fucking waiting fans going down the fucking street and round the fucking corner. You is still one mother fucking miserable cunt sucking mother fucker. Right?

D; Right.

A; So...maybe...just maybe... you was aksing... you was aksing... the wrong fucking question. Right?

D; Well... maybe... right.

A; A better question to aks would have been, like fucking, 'what will make me happy'? And going out and fucking looking for the right answer out there, everywhere except up your fucking cunt. Coz that didn't fucking work. You aint happy. Right? Right? And now, you gots a mother fucking cock the size of King Neptune. And, you still aint fucking happy.

*All get up. S goes to the piano and starts to play a
tune.*

He's fucked up.
The fucking cunt confessed it so its true.
He fucked up.
He fucking dunt know what to fucking do.

The doctors smiled at the money.
The nurses smiled at the girl.
Then they cut out all her honey
And stapled on his kingly burl.

He was a girl. He was a girl.
Now he is a man it's all a whirl.
Not happy with his titties.
Not happy with his cunt.
Not happy with the shitties
Now he's just another grunt.

He's fucked up.
The fucking cunt confessed it so its true.
He fucked up.
He fucking dunt know what to fucking do.

D is put in the middle of the stage and they all dance round him slapping him, taunting him and calling him 'fucker' and anything they think of. E brings out more coffee and they all sit round the table except Denny who stays alone centre stage.

A; Denny boy-girl. Dub. You played your fucking hand and lost. Life don't owe any one or all of us shit and then we go. Who the fuck is it that you want to be proud of you fucker? Your mother? Your father? You don't know them! But... but... here and now... you is still one mother fucking fucked up family cunt to us.

All; Ole!

A: Look at us, Dub. Look good and see us for maybe the first time boy. We is all fucked up. Stevey boy, and Emma the bi bitch, and Boris the fuck head, and Carl the creepy crapper. We is shit on the wind. We is mother fucking losers from on high till the dirt fills our fucking mouths. All we gots is now. This shit right here. And you would all agree, shitters, that this is perfect fucking shit-yeah?

All: Yeah. Creamy juicy brown bowling super shit of shit.

A; We is all learned something we didn't know before today. We know to aks questions. Or you wouldn't be talking to us about this shit, eh?

D: Yeah. Right. I knew something was fucked up. Now what I know… I can see it… it's me. Now I fucking know. Shit on me. Now I know. I'm the one whats fucked up. I always was. I went short when I should've gone long. The answer was that I was full of shit before, and ho ho ho, I still am. Fuck me. Fuck me over a beggar shitter's fucking barrel. I fucking fucked up. Shit shit shit. Hah. I feel better. Not much but I do feel better I can tell. Fucking mother fucking fuckers. What the fucking hell. I gots me a fucked up mother fucking family who don't give a fucking shit for me and I don't give a fucking shit for them.

A; Ring that fucking bell.

All; Ole!

D; Then why do you spend time with me eh? Your fucking choices. You can fucking walk away. Any fucking time. Any fucking day.

A; Why…?

S; Coz we is all as fucked up as you is Denny. We don't even deserve each other. We get ass fucked a 100 times a day. We don't know nothin. We just hang on the nose of the next fuck up. Together.

A; We don't know no fucking better.

E; That's family. That is it right there. Uhuh. Fucking family.

B; Family in the ass of the fucking food chain.

C; Lookin up. We is fucking looking up and up.

B; Talking about looking up, I'm going to sell this shit we got. Carl, Denny, fucking out. I want some fam-i-ly holding up my ass when we see the Fat Man and sell this crap.

E; You're going to see Momo?

B; Yeah. Today. Its been another day of shit and now this new shit- questions. I want to sell this shit gone and THEN think about some more questions.

B makes a text message.

C; This question shit. Its big. I mean, fucking A big. Up and up.

A; Right.

S; Right.

E; Right.

D; Fuck heads… I want to tell you something. I… I… like you.

All; Ole!

S; Well fuck me ass blind in a bag. Denny likes us.

E: Yeah. Fuck.

B; Who the fuck could have known that mother fucker?

A; You you fucker, is one of us. One of us. Family fucker. The fucking fuck head family.

C; Aha. The family fuck of fucking fuck heads!

A; Denny the mother fucker fuck head.

E; Denny- Dub the fuck head.

S; on piano plays along...
All (*except Denny*);

Denny the fuck head of the fuck head family.
Denny the fuck head likes fucking you and me.
Denny oh Denny hates his fucking self.
He hung his fucking pussy up on the fucking shelf,
Denny oh Denny who hates his fucking self.
And for us its fucking fuck head Denny
Who fucks the mother fuckers any fucking way.
Denny the fuck head of the fuck head family.
Denny the fuck head likes fucking you and me.

All (*except Denny*);
Yay. Yah. Woo. Hey. Woof woof woof.

D; Alright, alright. Dub's done now, fucking tough.
It's fucking done enough alright. Enough.

S; Denny, you's what we call 'fucked in the head'.
Same as all of us.

B; Mother fucking dead.

E; I jams my fizzle whizzle on at any time I can.

S; I don't do fucking nothing coz that's who the
fuck I am.

A; I fuck any fucker with 'victim' tattooed on their
brow.

B; I fuck any body live, dead or either beef or cow.

C; I'll fuck up your juicy brown bowl ass be you girl
or man.

E; And we'll keep on fucking doing it 'til we change
our plans.

All;
We'll all fucking fuck you, hood up
and take you to your grave.
Then we'll drink your fucking blood up
and fuck off to a rave.

B; You are a mother fucking fucker.
Ok? You is we.

Our fucking same assed mother fucker
Fucker you 'n' me.

Finish with applause and whistle and whoops.

B; Ok. Dub? Done, fucker. C'mon, lets go. Momo's local now.

B, C and D go to exit stage cafe door with some bags.

A; Me an Stevey 'll come with. I wants to aks Momo a que-st-i-on.

A & S follow out

SCENE FOUR

E takes a broom and brushes round the floor. Then she turns on some music.

Wistful. She plays with her phone a bit, texts in and out. As she sweeps to the music she sings...

There was a time
As a young girl
I had a jewel box
Of paper and pearl.

A cheap little box
That sat by my bed.
Empty to look in
But magic instead.

I'd open and wonder
Where I kept my dreams
I'd see and I'd ponder
All my hopes and my schemes.

How can I tell Stevey?
He's a fucker like the rest.
How can I tell Stevey
He's a father- he's so messed?

One day I'd be
With family
And then I'd know
What Love was so.

This morning I tested
And up came the blue
This morning I bested
My dream's coming true.

How can I tell Stevey?
He's a fucker like the rest.
How can I tell Stevey
He's a father- he's so messed?

What can I do with fuckers and with scum?
Family is family for whatsoever comes.
Stevey aint gonna make to settle.
He wont change his way anyhow.
My man aint got the shake of metal
He'll mess through each day any now.

How can I tell Stevey?
He's a fucker like the rest.
How can I tell Stevey
He's a father- he's so messed?

Did I think it would be so easy?
I don't know what to do.
I'll have to sit down with the sleaze see,
And try to talk it though.

How will I tell Stevey?
He's a fucker like the rest.
How will I tell Stevey
He's a father- he's so messed?

He's a mess. He's a mess.
He's a fucking fucked up fucking mess.
He's a mess. He's a mess.
His mess, my mess, our mess. It's a mess.

Song finishes and S and A come back in.

A: Emma...?

E; I'll get some coffee.

S; **I'll** get the coffee. And toasties. You sit down, Emma. Andy wants to ask you a fucking que-st-i-on.

E; So- fucking what fuck face?

A; Do you remember when we did that concert out at Brady Field? The rock thing?

E; Yeah. Yeah. I do.

A; We did good then. Pulled in 10 clear after all for a few hours of shine.

E; So- fucking what?

A; There's a bigger concert in a few days. Saturday night. Some singer there. Same venue. You want to come in? I'm gonna let Stevey come.

E; Oh yeah. Oh. Wait. No. I- I cant.

A; What the fuck. You got religion or fucking something?

E; Well...hah. What date is Saturday?

A; No fucking idea.

E; Just check... Oh well. Should be OK. What times? I have to close the cafe.

A; Dunno. It'll be evening times I suppose. Only need max three hours and fucking shwoosh shwoosh shwoosh.

E; Andy...

A; What?

E; I- oh- nothing. Fucking nothing.

S; Here we go. Fucking coffee with toasties. Fucking perfect. Minus bi spit.

E; Woh. Good shit, Stevey. Thanks.

S; A thanks? From you? Fuck. I should get it stuffed, fuck it and mounted on the fucking wall.
A; Hahaha. Fuck, Emma, you're passive after all we been through this fucking morning. You gonna roll over so Stevey can tickle your fucking belly?

E; Maybe I fucking will at that, cunt face.

E gets up and exits stage left.

A: Stevey. Things are fucking changing. There's some kind of fresh wind in the air. It feels like the

first day of Spring after a damn shitty Winter
somehow and I fucking don't get it.

S; You feel that? Fuck. I feel it too.
It's like something is coming. Something new.
Something good. Something better. Fuck you.

S; goes to the piano and plays. A sings.

A;
I only give a shit a lonely little bit.
It's all a fuck up any ways I looks at it.
It used to be so fucking great-
Fucking shitters were my dates-
It used to be so fucking great
Fucking shitters with my hate.

What's the game? What's the game?
This fucking new obliging is so lame.
What's the game? What's the game?
I'm a pussy dickless shitter- all the same.
What's the game? What's the game?
This fucking new me pussy's just insane.

I used to fly such an adrenalin high
The sun at my back and the wind in my eye.
Any time, any day,
I was up and away

but why?

Why can't I rip off my fucking brother?
Why don't I fucking want to steal?
Why can't I fuck my shitty sister?
What the fuck is fucking wrong
with the fucking way I fucking feel?

What's the game? What's the game?
This fucking new obliging is so lame.
What's the game? What's the game?
I'm a pussy dickless shitter- all the same.
What's the game? What's the game?
This fucking new me pussy's just insane.

I was flying never falling, not a care.
Ripping off of any shitters any where.
Now me's gone 'n' fucking flew off up out there.

What's the game? What's the game?
This fucking new obliging is so lame.
What's the game? What's the game?
I'm a pussy dickless shitter- all the same.
What's the game? What's the game?
This fucking new me pussy's just insane.

What the fuck. Don't ask Andy what he found.
Me 'n' Andy flew shit any wheres around
But I blew me off, lost me on the ground.

What's the game? What's the game?
This fucking new obliging is so lame.
What's the game? What's the game?
I'm a pussy dickless shitter- all the same.
What's the game? What's the game?
This fucking new me pussy's just insane.

I fucking let me go my fucking hand
and
Crashed Andy's shitting space ship on the land.
News is, I'm fucking grounded, understand?

Why cant I rip off my fucking brother?
Why don't I fucking want to steal?
Why cant I fuck my shitty sister?
What the fuck is fucking wrong
With the fucking way I fucking feel?

What's the game? What's the game?
This fucking new obliging is so lame.
What's the game? What's the game?

I'm a pussy dickless shitter just the same.
What's the game? What's the game?
This fucking new me pussy's just insane.

S; and A sit at the table.

S; You is sure fucked up with this new ques-ti-on
fucking shit, bro.

A; Yeah. Yeah. I am. It's like it had to come, though.
It's like it's been growing inside of me without a
sound- without letting on- like a fucking secret
pregnant woman- for a long time, and today- you
know- it's a kind of fucking birth day. Yeah. A
fucking birthday. When I woke up today, it was
there, inside, like- bursting, ready to pop. Then I
came here and- BOOM. I feel like I just had a
fucking baby right here with you all fuck heads.
We should celebrate or something. When the
others get back, yeah?

S; Yeah. Great idea, fuck head. Great idea. You is
the papa of the big fucking idea. The up and up.
The questionater. The asker master. The who is
blew is. Andy had a baby. Andy had a baby. Andy
had a baby and he fucking fucked hisself.

A; Maybe so... maybe so. I'm still just another fuck head though. But, I is trying. I is trying.

S; Hahaha. Just so. But, Andy. Tell me. Bro. What the fuck... is that weird thing in your bag then?

A; Ah.

S; Ha.

A; Ah.

S; Ha.

A; Ah ha.

S; Ah ha fucking ha ha ha.

A; Look. Stevey boy. It's like this. It's ... like... I don't fucking know.

S; But you know what it MEANs, yeah?

A; Yeah. Yeah. It means ask questions and don't listen to lies or any fuck shit from any fucking mother fucking lying cunting shitter.

S; Yeah....

A; And stop taking it up the ass.

S; Yeah…And?

A; And…

S; Yeah… And?

A; And? And. And… go… up.

S; What you mean, 'go up'?

A; I mean, go, get better. Do good shit. Don't do bad shit. Don't let shitters piss in your mouth, and don't piss in theirs, unless they piss in yours first. In which case, fuck 'em.

S; So, all the shitters who been pissing in our mouths, right?

A; Yeah.
S; And all these shitters who been fucking our juicy brown bowls, right?

A; Yeah.

S; We get a freebie to fuck them all, right?

A; Yeah. As Emma said, right, they been raping us for as long as we been alive. With lies that they spin out so sweet you can candy a year's supply of fucking cotton with just one.

S; Fuck. Them shitters is full of it all right. Ain't that the truth of it. Hmm... Truth... Big juicy brown bowling truth.... Hmm.

A; Talking of which... be right back.

A exits stage right. After a moment E walks in and sits down coyly next to S.

E; Stevey...

S; Emma...

E; How you feeling fuck head, huh? You ok?

S; Yeah. Um...*(coughs)*. Fuck. How are you feeling, Emma? Fuck head?

E; I'm good, fuck head.

S; Emma.

E; Yeah?

S; Why is you smiling at me like that?

E; I wasn't.

S; Yeah you was. Smiling. Kinda sideways.

E; Nah.

S; Yeah.

E; Nah.

S; Yeah.

E; Well not so I'd noticed.

S; This new thing. Like. Fuck head. Wah.

E; What new thing?

S; This new way of oblig- ing-ness- gation.

E; What?

S; I'm trying it out, see. This is me, trying it out. OK? Emma, hows you feeling today, huh?

E; Ah. I see. Yeah. Right. Hmm. Try it some more.

S; OK. How's this? Good morning, Emma. How are you today?

E; Wow. Fucking A. I mean... I'm fine thanks. How are you?

S; I'm just fucking A. Oh. I mean.. I'm fine thanks. May I pour you some coffee?

E; Wo. Wo. I think...it suits you, Stevey boy.

S; SUITS me?

E; Yeah. It makes you come across like more of a man. More... mature. Schooled. Clevererer. Respectablazed.

S; Respectablazed?
E; Yeah. That.

S; Foor. Woo. Wow. Respectablazed.

E; Yeah. Like you mean something. Something bigger than you were, yesterday. Last week. Before. Bigger and better. Like, you have this secret idea that tomorrow matters just as much as today, and you aint gonna fuck it up.

S; Holy crap. I... Listen. Andy and I was talking just now, an he says, right, he says, that he feels like he fucking had a baby today. With all this new crap and stuff we been talking about, you know?

E; Yeah I think I do know.

S; A baby. For fucks sake. I mean, who does shit like having a fucking baby these fucking crappy days, huh?

E takes S's hand and smiles into his eyes.

S; Oh fuck. No. Oh fuck no. Oh fucking fuck no no no no no.

E; Blue. 3 months. Don't know. Could be either.

S falls back onto the floor and looks up at the roof. Talks from the floor.

S; Fuck. Fuck. Fuck...You know, Emma, you should come down here and look up for a bit. Shit looks so different from down here.

E lies down next to S and looks up at the roof.

E; Yeah. I see what you mean. It's a fucking roof.

S; No, come on. We is always looking sideways. Never up. Its how our eyes are, Emma. Fucking sideways. Take this view, right-

E; The roof?

S;- and see it with your mind from the ground up.

E; I like it. I think I see what you mean.

S; Yeah. Look.

E; It's so... roofy.

S; I know you know what I mean and you can see it. Quit fucking me around.

E; Aw, I wouldn't do that to you, Stevey.

S; Fuck, wouldn't you.

E; Fuck you.

S; Fuck you.

E; Fuck you.

S; Fuck you.

S; Are you fucking with me, Emma?

E; No. It's real. Really real.

S; Fuck me. Really real?

E; Yeah. Really real.

S; Fuck you.

E; Fuck you.

S; Fuck you.

E; Fuck you.

S: Fuck you.

E and S. On the floor. They hit each other around the shoulders and shout 'FUCK YOU' at each other. Over and over. Then they grab each other and wrestle and scream and shout. Then they kiss.

S is on top and pulls away looking down at E.

S; Are you fucking with me Emma?

E; No. But that is why I is stuffed now. Fuck head.
Your freewizzle was working good, Stevey boy.

SCENE FIVE

A enters.

A; Fuck me what a mess.

S & E; Yeah. Yeah.

B, C and D enter through the cafe door.

B; Heya, fuckheads.

All sit at the table they drink coffee and smile.

A; So?

B; Ah. You know, Momo's a mother fucker.

He plops a bundle of cash on the table.

A; That's all?

B; Two and half. Plus what we had in cash before.

A; He is a mother fucker, sure.

B; Yeah. We pushed it hard, too.

S; That fucker's shitting on us from on fucking high.

A; Yeah. He's a fucking juicy brown bowling mother fucker.

C; That's why people call him 'the fat man'.

D; He owns more property round here than anyone. Rents it all out. Makes a fucking bundle every fucking day.

E; I hate him.

All; We all hates Momo.

E; He just sits on our heads and takes money from everyone.

C; Yeah. Fuck Momo.

A; Yeah. Let's do ourselves a great big favour and forget about that mother fucker. Fellow fuck head family. Today, we is having us a celebration. Today is a special birthday.

*S goes to piano and starts playing happy
tune. They all stand centre stage.*

A;
Before, before
We was at fucking war.
We fucked it up and messed life all around.
Today. Today
We made a fucking move that's fucking sound.

All:
Happy birthday to our futures.
Happy birthday to new thoughts.
Happy birthday to a weird thing
And to the changes it has brought.

A;
We saw. We saw.
The difference turned out being fucking plain.
So now. So now.
We shan't take it up the fucking ass again.

All;
Happy birthday to our futures.
Happy birthday to new thoughts.
Happy birthday to a weird thing
And to the changes it has brought.

A;
Its true. Its true.
We're learning how to fucking think with brains.
We do. We do
We question everything we're told like rain.

All;
Happy birthday to our futures.
Happy birthday to new thoughts.
Happy birthday to a weird thing
And to the changes it has brought.

A;
They will. They will
They'll lie us down with any crap we hear.
We won't. We wont
Believe them 'til our fucking minds are clear.

All:
Happy birthday to our futures.
Happy birthday to new thoughts.
Happy birthday to a weird thing
And to the changes it has brought.

A;
Although. Although
It's each one of us that's got to think alone.
We know. We know
A family helps to know what's gold or stone.

All;
Happy birthday to our futures.
Happy birthday to new thoughts.
Happy birthday to a weird thing
And to the changes it has brought.

Talking while S is playing;

S;
We fucking well don't know shit.

A; That's a great floor to start walking on.

All;
We is brain babies mother fucker.

B; Fuck all this climbing change shit.

C; Yeah. Fuck all this juicy brown bowl ass fucking.

E; Yeah. Family is the mostest thing up there.

All;
To fucking die for!

S; We is going up respectiblazes.

E; Yeah. Get a job.

B; Yeah. Get a life.

C; Yeah. Make some serious changes.

D; Yeah. Yeah. I'm gonna do it. Serious. Fuck my issues. Fuck me. I'm gonna start a business. Helping people who are sick. Doing their cleaning. Shopping. Cooking. Fixing shit in their homes. Old people. Young people. Needy, sick people who have problems doing stuff I know is fucking easy. I is going to be wanted. Needed. For what I do-not for who I am.

All Singing

Happy birthday to our futures.
Happy birthday to new thoughts.
Happy birthday to a weird thing
And to the changes it has brought.

Happy birthday to our futures.
Happy birthday to new thoughts.
Happy birthday to a weird thing
And to the changes it has brought.

While all this singing is going on, a series of ropes with hooks come down from the roof. They all hook onto one each, and get lifted up into the stage roof as the (added)music and singing play out.

....

COPYRIGHT NOTICE

DON'T FUCKING ABUSE PEOPLE'S RIGHTS.

I aint popping over my ass so you can slide a few in mother fucker. Fuck you.

You do that to me, that means I get to do that shit to you fucker. I aint known for my merciful nature, fuck heads. ***Be fucking warned.***

Email in each instance for any copyright requirement prior to any use. Fees may apply for licensing in any and all circumstances at the sole and final discretion of the copyright owner.

In the first Instance:- Email:-
Mr Larry Higgins
higginslarry324 (at) gmail.com

This email address may be updated from time to time depending on the fucking world fucking changing every ten fucking minutes.

IMPORTANT NOTICE. PLEASE READ CAREFULLY.

COPYRIGHT APPERTAINING TO THIS ORIGINAL INTELLECTUAL PROPERTY UNDER USA LAW.

What Is a Copyright?
All works, whether published or unpublished, are protected by copyright. The copyright may be held by an individual or by a company representing the playwright, publisher, or composer.

Licensing Fees and Royalties

Performing a work, whether a play script or musical score, is prohibited without receiving permission from the copyright holder, and in most cases paying a licensing fee and/or royalties. Fees and royalties are determined by the seating capacity of the theater, number of scripts ordered, number of performances, and ticket prices.

Keep in mind that musical compositions are protected in a slightly different manner in that the rights also include control over use in a public performance. "Performance" is defined rather broadly and can be taken to mean a classroom as well as a theater or other performance space, so even if you are using the music for a classroom performance that is not "open to the public," it is necessary to obtain written permission and probably pay a fee to use the music.

The copyright holder reserves the right to complete and entire control for the public use of the work in every sense and in part, parts and in whole, at any time, for any number of times and for any reasons. Hence why written permission and an agreed licence and fees need firstly be formally agreed and contracted with limitations prior to any form of use.

'Fair use' laws applying to the sampling, reference to and distribution of any part, parts or the whole of the work is prohibited without firstly having formal written consent in contract agreed by all concerned parties to the intended action. Accidental, negligent or ignorant distribution of the work in any part, part or parts is subject to the same regulated permission required and may be enforced retrospectively with penalties for abuse of copyright holder's privileges.

Can I Change the Script or Words to a Song?

Simply put, no—not unless you receive written permission from the company or individual holding the rights. In other words, you cannot arbitrarily alter the words in a script or the words to a song to suit your school's needs without first contacting the copyright holder.

Can I Record the Event?

In general, personal recordings of your child acting or singing taken with your video camera are fine, but if a school wants to make an official recording of a play or performance and show it on say, the local cable channel, then permission must be requested and granted. If anyone (legal entity) wishes make and then to use a public recorded performance for any purposes commercial, social, intellectual or for any form of catalogue, then prior approval for the specific action(s) MUST be first obtained from the copyright holder, and may be subject to licensing fees in their sole and final discretion.

What If Our School Can't Afford to Pay Fees and Royalties?

If your school doesn't have the money to pay for royalty or licensing fees, then consider using material that has entered into the public domain and is free from copyright protection.

The rules regarding public domain, however, can be somewhat tricky. Works published on or before January 1, 1923 are considered to be in the public domain. Works published between 1923 and 1977 that did not contain a valid copyright notice and works published between 1923 and 1963 with notice, but whose copyrights weren't renewed are also part of the public domain. Works created between 1964 and 1977 and published with copyright notice are protected in the US until 95 years after the date of the initial publication; however, works published in the

US with copyright notice on or after January 1, 1978 are protected by copyright for 70 years after the author's death. There are additional conditions in many cases, so be sure to check the US Copyright website for public domain details.

The bottom line is that if you are not sure whether the song, play script, or anything else is protected by copyright, it pays to find out. With fines for copyright infringement ranging from $500 to $100,000 or more, copyright infringement is serious business and should not be taken lightly by anyone.

Licensing fees for the legal category of 'performance' of **this work** under USA copyright law:-

1/. Reproduction.

To reproduce this work in any electronic or printed format without the prior written consent, contract and agreement of the copyright owner is open to civil action and penalty in law for commercial intellectual property abuse and damage through losses. If any legal entity should require one or more printed copy of this work in part, parts and/or in whole, the correct procedure currently agreed by the copyright owner that is open to successful and honest acquisition, is to buy each full copy of the work from the contracted sources of distribution at the time. Such distribution sources may change from time to time at the sole and final discretion of the copyright owner without any prior specific notice or public notification through any media or format.

2/. Performance.

Performance of this work is limited by the rights of the copyright owner in every context; be it private, public, commercial, social or intellectual. For specific details and in every event of intended use prior, it is legally required that any natural person, persons and/or legal entity obtain agreement by contract for specific and limited use in part, parts and in whole, for which fees shall be due and payable to the copyright owner. Such limited contracts are not transferable, have no inherent value to the license holder and cannot be used for any financial purposes outside those therein by limited and agreed prior, and all due fees being paid and up to the specific moment prior to the start of every performance on its date as agreed.

Email (as above) to the copyright holder explaining your every intention for each instance to begin the process of agreement for licensing and fee payments.

3/. For licensing and performance outside the USA, please write too the copyright holder in the first instance and enquire in exactly the same procedure as if the intended use was for inside the USA.

4/. If in any doubt, email the copyright owner before you take your next breath.

FUCK YOU SHITTERS

Some information about the author.

Ulrick Yczeniaplaus was born. As this was without his consent, he was pissed then and still is now. Still, being stuck with the life he got, he deals with it in the usual way. Being pissed. Staying pissed. Getting pissed and remaining pissed for as long as possible without the need to be sober, articulate, thoughtful or clever.

Preferences:-

He prefers the company of his dearest friend to any other- the wall. Not any wall, you understand, but only the one he happens to be nearest to at the time.

Likes:-

Drooling is good; specially in front of people in authority. He likes to accompany this with the most vacant stare he can muster.

Dislikes:-

He does not like, appreciate or ask for any kind of person in authority to stick their cocks up his ass; a part of his body absolutely reserved for the single action nature intended it for; juicy brown bowling deprecation.